THE CONFESSIONS

CARMAS MCLAUGHLIN

Copyright © 2021 by Carmas Mclaughlin

All rights reserved. No part of this publication may be reproduced, distributed, or transmitted in any form or by any means, including photocopying, recording, or other electronic or mechanical methods, without the prior written permission of the publisher, except in the case brief quotations embodied in critical reviews and other noncommercial uses permitted by copyright law.

ISBN: 978-1-954341-07-4 (Paperback)

The views expressed in this book are solely those of the author and do not necessarily reflect the views of the publisher, and the publisher hereby disclaims any responsibility for them.

Writers' Branding
1800-608-6550
www.writersbranding.com
orders@writersbranding.com

Contents

Special thanks iv
A Rose That Grew Out Of Concrete 1
A Rose Confession 2
Angles 4
Angle Confession 5
Demons 7
Demons Confession 8
Hate You 10
Hate You Confession 11
Honey 13
Honey Confessions 14
No Good Deed 16
No Good Deed Confession 17
No Trespassing After Dark 19
No Trespassing After Dark Confession 20
If I Had One Wish 22
One Wish Confession 23
Politics Of Life 25
Politics Confession 26
Possessions 28
Possessions Confession 29
Sick Of Yo Shit 31
Sick of Yo Sick Confession 32
Temptations 34
Temptation Confession 35
Just Text Me 37
Text Me Confession 38
Wet Dreams 40
Wet Dreams Confession 41
While You Were Out 43
While You Were Out Confession 44

Special thanks

Thank you — Demetrius jackson, Bryant Bennette, Jenae Mayo. To my mother — Gloria Mclaughlin
To my father — Cecil Mclaughlin
In addition, a few other friends. Thanks for believing in me.

Thanks Xlibris and the wonderful team that helped me get through another chapter in my life.

A Rose That Grew Out Of Concrete

It was a struggle, it was hard.
The rain and storms always beat you up but keep standing.
Your roots were pushed threw the side walks.
Coming up was not a cake walk for you.
The children played hot scotch around you but, you keep on letting the sunlight in.
I see your scars but can you be fixed.
You were a different kind of flower.
Your eyes were like cold steal.
Your beauty was alien to this world.
Your strength withstood all four seasons.
I would harvest the and place you in a beautiful vase with fresh water.
I would build your dreams with my two hands.
It was what I wanted but you're not for me.
We were too different. Even though I watered you, but I was yet to be weathered out.

A Rose Confession

Have you ever watched a woman strugle to make ends meet? Have you ever wondered why some women seem so bitter?
If you only knew what hell, they seen from the time they were child to an adult.
Sometimes they turn out good and sometimes just bitter.
A true rose that grew out of concrete will always be a strong woman.

Notes

Angles

When I came, you was there.
If it wasn't for your eyes, then I would have never knew.
I notice you watching me. I feel your heart piercing mine.
When I look at you, I don't see you but I see a Goddess.
Take my hand in yours and I'll place my other on top of yours.
I stare at the beauty of your lips.
I am comforted by the words you speak.
Embrace me in your arms and I will behold you in mine. Your tongue melted like words in my mouth.
I fell asleep in a room of darkness and you lit the room up with your presence.
I reached out my hand and said lady's first.
You were my guide and my light.
Will you take me I asked?
My angle said to me, only if you ask me first.
And together we were standing under the ark.

Angle Confession

Sometimes in your life, you meet people that bring only light to your life. Have somebody ever got your attention and you couldn't focus on nothing but there best interest.
The only thing you see is the good.

Notes

Demons

I hear you calling me but I don't want it.
I was up a trance and I couldn't shake it off.
I felt your hands on my back and every time I turn around, nothing is there. I feel your touch all over my body.
I just can't resist how my body tingles and explode with the slightest touch of your hands.
Just whisper and I'll catch your breath.
Just me and you and nobody else suppose to be here.
If I can just walk away from your arms.
Its just that you cool me off like ice on pissed on pop sickles. But my body burns from the inside out. The earge just want go away.
Come and lay with me just one more time.
I cry as I feel your wrath in my veins. Then everything went dark.

Demons Confession

Some things don't need an explanation.
An addiction is a addiction.
It can be drugs,alcohol,sex,or whatever.
Some people just need prayer.

Notes

Hate You

Then curse you, I already told you.
I don't like you.
I don't know why I feel this way.
I just hate you.
Maybe its a stage, a mood swing right now.
Maybe, I'm just not feeling you.
I use to like you but now, I despise you.
You use to rub my back, you use to pop my zits, baked my favorite dish.
Now you just a memory, a has been, a sweetness that turned bitter.
Just the imagination that I left in my sleep, it was a nightmare.
A thin line between love and hate indeed.
I wish I never found you or did you find me.
I don't remember how I met you.
What the hell you do to me
All I know is, I hate you.

Hate You Confession

I once reached my breaking point with someone.
I tried my hardest to love but then it was complete opposite. It was just at the point of no return.
Hate and love is like a magnet, a negative and a positive therefore that line is thine between love and hate. Would I be lying to say opposites attract.

Notes

Honey

It was sweet
It was sticky
It was slick coated
It wasn't sour
It was honey
It tasted real good
My mouth was watery
It was all over my face
It was shiny
It was honey
I wanted more
It was delicious
I got closer and closer
Honey came out more and more
Sweet barbeque sauce all over my face
Wrap them around my head
That nectar on my tongue
Sweet honey mustard
It was on my chin
It was in my beard
It was honey baby.

Honey Confessions

What is understood don't need to be explained.

Notes

No Good Deed

It was a darn shame when the window fell out.
My eyes were affixed on the inbox.
It's a time for everything and not a time to forget my gloves.
The alarm didn't trip and I'll
say that's no good deed. Thankfully I
at all the wires the night before.
My mine was made and my fate was
sealed. No time to turn back now.
Whoops, I didn't know that all was asleep,
but I'll make sure anyway.
Hammers always come in handy. Now I'll say
that's no good deed. I just want my
hands on the prize.
Looks like a propane tank over there
beside a gas stove. Oh how convenient.
On my way out now. I guess hammerhead
Want be needing this anymore.
Like a thief in the night.
All I thought was, diamonds are beautiful
and then I heard kaboom.

No Good Deed Confession

I tell you, nothing good can come from anything that's bad.
Plead the 5th.
We all plead the 5th.
Somebody plead the 5th please.
witch amendment was that again?

Notes

No Trespassing After Dark

Once upon a time I stepped out on a limb.
Life was like Nascars.
around and Around, repetition offer repetition.
I was standing still and the world was still spinning faster and faster.
I was running on empty.
I Passed out and then I begin to dream.
I was awaken in a room of darkness and it had no walls.
I felt a breeze and I heard crackling under my feet.
Life no longer tasted sweet. this can't be right, I'am not suppose to be here.
Then I saw a transparent fogger and it begin to point at a door way behind me, I asked, "What is it " this is the door to the world you missed, the one you never noticed.
Right now, you are trespassing. Slow down before the branch breaks under you.

No Trespassing After Dark Confession

When I was a younger man,
I didn't care about the future.
I just wanted the now.
I was living my life fast.
Do it now and think about it later.
One day, I met my son.
Then I begin to see things different.
Everything changed, I started to dream different.
I saw a new purpose again.
I got quiet then I started making a different noise.

Notes

If I Had One Wish

If I had one wish.
I would hold it with both my hands.
I wouldn't waste it . I want abuse it.
I want rush it.
I'll take my time with it.
Just one wish.
Motivate me, inspire me, just touch me.
I wouldn't worry about making it twice.
I wouldn't risk a mistake.
Just one wish.
It would be like a fragile air bubble.
It would descend slowly from the sky and I would catch it. I would carefully close my eyes.
Thoughts roll from the back of my mine and I would choose just one.
If I had one wish,
I would wish for you.

One Wish Confession

Its like I dated all the bad apples.
You go in thinking corner and you just think about everything in the world that you can possibly want and have.
You sum it all down to one thing.
If you can have that one perfect person or that perfect something you always wanted, what would be your one wish?

Notes

Politics Of Life

It was nature when it was written .
It was the cold and it was the warmth.
It gave me thought and then I was thinking.
I was in a trance but I was comfortable.
It was already written.
This was just the law.
Everything was in order.
The birds cut through the wind and the wind cut through my lungs.
It was all like nature and everything was understood.
Everything has its purpose, some vague and others clear. Man have his flesh and animal have its fur. In a political world, you can argue with that.
But these are just the politics of.
this is my world.

Politics Confession

The politics, they were all thoughts from my mind and all things a part of life.
Everything has its purpose.
The world itself have its reason for existence.
If you were an alcoholic, then I am pretty darn sure that you got your reason for doing it.
the title, Politics of Life contained situations of life's circumstances.

Notes

Possessions

I gotta have this,l this is gold, this is what's right.
This shit is mine.
I'll be domed if I let you go.
My pride, the lust, this whole place.
This is my kingdom and there ain't gonna be no negotiations.
Manifest on my words.
I'm the elicte, the enlighten. How much longer will it be.
Like a bride, bring it, walk with it, and relinquish it.
I bolster what I have.
Don't be mad, for this shit is mine.
Oh thank you, did you, give me that.
I can just take it. I feel like I earned it. It all became clear.
It's simple, it's just my positions.

Possessions Confession

People will do just about anything for money.
Sometimes it becomes just pure greed.
The power of it.
Money can't buy love but, it sure is hell increase your odds.

Notes

Sick Of Yo Shit

I got so tired of waiting, I just couldn't think.
I begin to puke up my feelings like mouth wash, I gargle and spit it out.
Running down the street like water in a drain.
You turned and saw me looking but it wasn't at you but past you.
I see a rainbow yesterday. And it had a new color in it.
It was black and was like a bird on a telephone wire that shitted and then it
was gone.
I needed you the most and you told me no but, you always offer me just to hear me say no.
What about what I need and what about what I want.
You entice me with what I don't need and give me what I don't want.
I'm just sick of yo shit.

Sick of Yo Sick Confession

I once got feed up with somebody that had my interest.
It seem like you can do everything to grab somebody's attention and they just ignore you until its convenient for them.
What if someone offered you something only because they knew you wouldn't accept.
One day you wake up and do it to them and they wonder what's going on.
Just tired of their shit and say hell with it.

Notes

Temptations

I try and look away but my eyes are caught.
Muscles were aching with pain but a dragon must be slain.
Like a rock was actually budging when it is already solid.
The table surface was caramel and brown but so oily and wet.
Two midgets on the bottom and the two water balloons on the top.
How can I resist when my mind was incarcerated. Only one-way out and that was with my key.
I watch the candle burn while the wax was dripping down on the table surface.
She took my sword and shined my blade.
The dragon must be slain but I tried to avoid such a dual. Slash after slash the beast was struck. Slash after perry and the tip was cut off. Like a eruption of a volcano, fire hurled out the dragons mouth. I watch her stare at me as I got up and walked away. In the end, I kept my key, for it was only temptations.

Temptation Confession

How tough was she I thought.
Is it truly a woman that dam gorgeous?
She was like a Goddess and she wanted me.
Her tits were amazing and I tell you, she had a dunk.
I walked into the room and she was soaked down
With body oil.
It was as if my mind was in a trance.
I started thinking about all the things I wanted to do to her.
I snapped back to reality.
I did have the opportunity but I walked away from it.

Notes

Just Text Me

I felt the vibration on my hip "wyd" I was on my
so I text right back.
I want come through if that's alright with you.
You need it from the store, I got you
You want be late. Will you still be awake.
I felt a vibration on my hip.
"I left the door unlocked"
Do not be late I just may be sleep.
Bring nothing more than a bag of plastic and a light tossed salad.
I was off my job so I text right back.
Before I leave the bank, I just wanna know is that thang gona bounce
because you already know not to write a check that your ass can't cash.
I'll be just a few.
So just text me back.

Text Me Confession

I was at work one afternoon.
This beautiful chick I met was texting me and I was texting her back and forth.
She was a dam diva. I was trying to hurry up and get off work.
Them eight hours couldn't come fast enough. She was kind of tired when I finally came over, but she was special because she waited on me. I liked her because she nasty, just the right kind and not that filthy nasty. I'm talking about that freak nasty.

Notes

Wet Dreams

I walked in the house and she was on the couch.
She was facing away
She was wearing a strawberry colored thong. The banana split was swallowing it.
I dropped all my bags.
Her juices where moistening as I drew closer. My mouth was drooling while I was unzipping.
I soaked my fingers in the bowel of jello.
It tasted so sweet and juicy.
The kitty was purring as I teased it with a snack.
The kitty cat was hungry so I feed it.
Hey kitty, I bet you can't eat just one.
My body dripped with sweat and hers was so oily wet.
Like a timer on a bomb, all the fluids were mixing.
Pumping like a pistol in a diesel engine, faster and faster and faster.
The cylinder begin to tighten then a sudden stop and BOOM!
An alarm was sounding, it was the phone "Hello, oh yeah, I was just waking up."
I'll see you in a 'lil bit.

Wet Dreams Confession

Some things that's understood, don't need to be explained.
but if I must I will.
Sometimes you might you just might have one of them dreams that's just too real.
So real, you can feel the flesh.
Don't you just hate when somebody wake you up and you can't go back again.
I'll say no more because what's understood, need not to be explained.

Notes

While You Were Out

While you were out, she put the coffee on. It was boiling hot.
So hot, you can hear the bubbles pop.
It was time to put the cream in it.
While you where out, she scrambled her on eggs.
She flipped and she tossed them just right.
She put the cheese in it. Nothing stuck because she had a lot of oil in it.
While you were out, she made her own sausage. She put the sausage in the eggs. It was a polish.
Dam, she got a lot of grease on.
Food was just everywhere.
While you where out, she did her own dishes.
She scrubbed them real good.
Three speed jets on the sink sprinkler.
Then you walked in
Dam where's your plate?
Ain't no coffee, ain't no eggs, ain't no sausage and just getting out the shower.
While you were out.

While You Were Out Confession

Well at lease you thought she was cooking.
Go home to your lady and you wonder why she was so calm, hmm.
You thought she was cheating but she wasn't
you might say something but she might go on defense because she don't wanna tell you what she was doing while you was out.
You come home looking for some loving but receive non because you had something better to.
While you was out she satisfied herself and now you assed out.

Notes

www.ingramcontent.com/pod-product-compliance
Lightning Source LLC
LaVergne TN
LVHW040202080526
838202LV00042B/3290